I Found Mouse

· ·

By Pamela D. Greenwood

Illustrated by
Jennifer Plecas

Clarion Books
New York

Clarion Books
a Houghton Mifflin Company imprint
215 Park Avenue South, New York, NY 10003
Text copyright © 1994 by Pamela Greenwood
Illustrations copyright © 1994 by Jennifer Plecas

The illustrations for this book were executed in pen and ink and watercolor
The text was set in 14/18 pt. Clearface

Book design by Sylvia Frezzolini
Printed in the USA

Library of Congress Cataloging-in-Publication Data
Greenwood, Pamela D.   I found Mouse / by Pamela D. Greenwood ; illus-
trated by Jennifer Plecas.   p.   cm.
Summary: When Mom goes away for three weeks, Tessie, Dad,
and their new kitten learn to take care of each other.
ISBN 0-395-65478-5
[1. Fathers and daughters—Fiction.   2. Cats—Fiction.]
I. Plecas, Jennifer, ill.   II. Title.
PZ7.G85324Iaf   1994   [Fic]—dc20   92-46427
                                              CIP
                                              AC
WOZ 10 9 8 7 6 5 4 3 2 1

For my daughters, Anna, Elisabeth, and Wynne.
P.D.G.

For Theresa and Tilly.
J.P.

CONTENTS

CHAPTER ONE
Mad at Mom

I was mad at Mom.

She was going to study Native American art this summer. In Colorado.

I sat on the end of the bed and watched her pack.

"Are you sure Mrs. Martin will take me to swim lessons?" I asked.

"She said she would, Tessie," Mom answered. "Willie's lessons are at the same time."

"What if Willie fights with me in the car?" I asked.

Mom raised her eyebrows. "Try to get along with Willie. Okay?"

"Four-year-olds are such babies," I said.

Mom tossed me some socks. "Can you fit these in the corners?"

I held the socks. Mom's hiking socks. I sighed and poked them into the suitcase.

"Are you sure Dad won't have to go to his office every day?" I asked.

"He may have to go in once in a while. But his boss agreed to let him work at home while I'm gone."

I ran my hands over Mom's silky red blouse.

"What if Mrs. Martin won't baby-sit me when Dad does have to go in because Willie and I fight in the car and fight in the house and keep the baby awake?"

Mom shook her head. "You're making it sound pretty bad."

"It *is* pretty bad," I said.

Mom sat down on the bed beside me. "I'll only be gone three weeks," she said. "This is a special chance for me. I know you can make it work out."

Later, Dad and Justin and I took Mom to the airport.
I gave her a goodbye hug. Even though I was still mad.
We stood at the window and watched the plane take off.
It got smaller and smaller. Pretty soon I couldn't see it.
"Time to go, Tessie," Dad said.
He let me sit in the front as we drove away.
I felt funny in the front seat. Like there was no mom
in our family anymore.

CHAPTER TWO

• • • • • • • • • • • •

Justin Leaves Too

We had to stop at the store on the way home. Justin needed some long underwear.

"It's summer," I said. "Everybody is wearing shorts."

"But I'll be in the woods," Justin said. "In the woods you have to be prepared for cold weather. Even in the summer."

Justin was leaving too. He was going on a backpack trip with Grandad.

We bought the long underwear and went home. I started to miss Justin and he wasn't even gone.

Mom called that night to tell us she got there safely. And to tell Dad she forgot to take the clothes out of the dryer.

She told Justin to have fun.

And she reminded me to get along with Willie Martin.

I need to have fun too, I thought.

Justin got up early the next morning. He double-checked his pack.

"I'm ready," he said.

Grandad brought us doughnuts for breakfast.

While we ate, he showed us on the map where they were going.

"Your turn is coming up, Tessie," he said to me, as Justin piled his things in the car. "You'll get to pick your own trail."

We all waved goodbye.

"Why can't I go now?" I asked Dad.

So he explained. Again.

"When I was ten, Grandad took me camping. Now Justin is ten, so Grandad is taking him. When you're ten, he'll take you."

"I wish I could go now," I said.

"Then who would take care of me?" Dad asked.

"Who is going to take care of *me*?" I asked back.

Dad laughed. "I guess we'll be taking care of each other."

CHAPTER THREE

. . . .

A Little Disorganized

There wasn't any milk for breakfast. Dad forgot to buy it.

"I can't eat my cereal without milk," I complained.

Mom wouldn't forget milk, I thought.

"How about the leftover doughnuts from yesterday?" Dad asked. He brought them over to the table.

They were stale and hard.

"Yuck," I said.

"I forgot to put them away," Dad said.

Mom wouldn't forget that either, I thought.

But I didn't have time for breakfast anyway. Willie Martin was pounding at the door.

"Hurry up," he shouted. "Mom says we'll be late."

"Where's my bag?" I shouted too.

"Didn't you pack it?" Dad asked.

"Nobody reminded me last night," I said.

I ran to get my swimsuit and Dad grabbed a towel from the closet.

"We're a little disorganized," Dad told Mrs. Martin when we got to the car. "We'll have the routine down tomorrow."

"I hate to be late," she said to Dad. "Buckle up," she said to me.

Willie and I were in different classes. Every time I looked over at him he was shaking his head. Once he hollered "No!"

"Why didn't you want to swim today?" Mrs. Martin asked Willie on our way back home.

Because I'm a baby. I mouthed the words for Willie to see.

"She called me a baby," he shouted.

I tried to look surprised.

Mrs. Martin glared.

Willie's baby brother, Kyle, started to cry.

Mrs. Martin sighed.

I found a note taped to our front door. It had
Mrs. Martin's name on it.

> *I had to go to the office to meet someone from
> out of town. Will you keep Tessie until I return?
> Thanks.*
>
> *Larry Walters*

Mrs. Martin sighed again.
We stayed outside so the baby could take his nap in peace.
We played on the swings. I stretched my legs up to the
sky and leaned my head back. The world was upside down.
"Push me," Willie said.

So I jumped off and pushed him.

"Higher," he shouted. "HIGHER!"

I pushed until I got tired.

"Keep pushing," Willie said.

But I quit. I stretched out in the shade under the willow tree.

Willie snuck up and squirted me with the hose, so I climbed up the tree. Out of Willie's reach. I stayed there till Dad picked me up.

"Willie Martin is a pain," I told him.

"I'm sorry this came up today," Dad said. "Things will get better."

CHAPTER FOUR

. . . .

I Miss Everybody

Things didn't get better the next day.

Dad said he'd take me to the park after lunch, but his boss called.

"I'm sorry," Dad told me. "I have to write a report this afternoon."

I wished it wasn't summer. Mom was gone. Justin was gone. Even my best friend, Mary Alice, was gone.

Mom thought Mary Alice would be home while she was away. But Mary Alice's dad and stepmom wanted her to visit them now instead of next month.

Mom said she was sorry, but she couldn't change the dates of the workshop.

Mom didn't care about my summer. That's why I was mad.

I got my stuffed animals out and started to play circus. But it wasn't much fun without Mary Alice.

I reread the postcard she sent me.

I got a new swim suit. My stepsister got one too.
We're going to Disney World next week.
Love, Mary Alice.
P. S. I miss my mom. And you.

When Mary Alice is there, she misses her mom. When she's here, she misses her dad.

Why did her dad leave home? I wondered. When did she know he wasn't coming back?

Mom called after dinner.
"Are you having fun?" she asked.
"No," I said.
"I'm working very hard," she said.
"So is Dad," I said.
"I miss you," she said.
"I miss everybody," I said.
I kept holding the phone after she hung up.
I pretended I was still talking to her.
"Are you sure you miss me?" I asked.
"Are you sure you're coming back?"

CHAPTER FIVE
. . . .

Colorado Is Spectacular

Thursday, Dad forgot dinner.

I was playing hopscotch for the hundredth time and my tummy started to growl.

I went in to ask Dad when we were going to eat.

He looked at his watch. Then he jumped up.

"It's six-thirty," he said. "I was so busy I forgot about dinner."

Dad opened the refrigerator. He shrugged. "How about pizza?"

Pizza used to be my favorite food. Till we had it four nights in a row.

But this time we went out to eat pizza instead of having it delivered.

"What else do you know how to cook?" I asked Dad.

Dad laughed. "Getting tired of pizza?"

I nodded.

"Don't forget my special-breakfast waffles."

"Can we have special-breakfast waffles for dinner? Tomorrow?"

"Why not?" Dad said.

The next time we talked to Mom, she told us about her hike.

"Some of us went to Mills Lake," she said. "It was spectacular."

"Does that mean you like Colorado better than here?" I asked.

"No. It just means I got to do some exploring."

"Are you going to stay in Colorado?" I asked.

"Not after the workshop is over," Mom said.

What if everything in Colorado is spectacular? I thought.

Dad and I went for a night walk.
I tried to match my steps to his long ones.
"What if Mom doesn't come back?" I asked him.
"She's coming back."
"What if she doesn't?" I said again.
Dad slowed down. "Mom will be back in two weeks."
"She's having a lot of fun exploring. What if she decides to stay there?"
"Mom is studying Native American art so she can be a better teacher back here," Dad said.

It was dark outside. We passed Mary Alice's house, and it was dark inside too.

"Mary Alice's dad didn't come back," I said.

Dad stopped and put his hands on my shoulders. "Is that why you're asking questions?"

"Yes," I whispered.

Dad took a deep breath. "I'm sorry that happened to Mary Alice. But it's not going to happen to you, Tessie." He gave me a big hug. "Mom will be back when her workshop is over."

CHAPTER SIX

· · · · · · · · · ·

Mouse

Sunday we went to the zoo.

We saw all my favorite animals. After our snack
I asked Dad if we could go to the snake house.

"I thought you didn't like the snakes," he said.

"But Justin does," I said. "If he were here, we'd go."

Dad smiled. "Let's go then."

We saw a new snake. A green tree python.

"Don't tell Justin about the snake," I said to Dad.
"Let's bring him here and surprise him."

"It'll be our secret," Dad said.

Then Monday morning Dad took us to swim lessons. Mrs. Martin had to take Kyle to get his shots.

Dad brought some papers to read. But every time I looked at him he was watching me instead of reading.

He even clapped when I dived off the diving board at the end of class.

When we got back home, Dad went straight to his desk and turned on the computer.

I still wished it wasn't summer. I sat outside and finished reading my last two books. Then I went back in.

"Let's go to the library." I walked over to Dad's desk and leaned on the corner. "I need some new books."

"I'm working right now." Dad didn't even look up. "Maybe we can go tonight."

"I'm bored," I said.

Dad gave me a little smile. "Well, find something to do."

I got my skates and went down the street.

I hoped Willie Martin wouldn't see me.

I passed his house like a comet.

There was no car in the driveway.

And no noise in the yard. Good.

Then I heard Mrs. O'Connor.

"Shoo," she said. "Shoo. Shoo. Shoo."

I saw a ball of gray fluff streak into the bushes.

Mrs. O'Connor shook her dust mop. "And don't come back."

She glanced at me. "Not you, Tessie. That scruffy stray cat. My George doesn't like him at all."

George swished his tail. "Do you, Georgie-porgie?"

George is fat. And stuck-up.

I waited till Mrs. O'Connor took George inside.

Then I knelt down and looked under the bushes.

"Meow. Meow," I said and held out my hand
to the gray kitty.

It backed up. Its eyes got wide.

"Don't be scared," I said. "I won't hurt you."

I finally had to crawl into the bush. I ducked under
the branches.

I got the kitty.

It wasn't a soft ball of fluff.

There were twigs in its fur. It had big ears. And
a skinny body. And a long skinny tail.

"You need something to eat," I said. "You look hungry."

I carried the kitty home. "I have just the name for you," I told it.

Dad was still at his desk.

"Meet Mouse," I said.

"A mouse in the house?" he said, looking at the computer screen.

Then he saw the kitty and chuckled. "Your Mouse is purring."

"What can it eat?" I asked.

Dad went to the kitchen. "How about cheese chunks?"

"Do cats like cheese?" I asked.

"Mice do." Dad laughed at his joke.

Mouse the cat gobbled the cheese. Dad cut more.

"Does Mouse have a home?" Dad asked.

"It does now," I said.

Dad shook his head. "We don't need a cat."

"You said find something to do," I said. "I found Mouse."

CHAPTER SEVEN

· · · · · · · · · · · ·

Lost and Found

Dad said we'd try it out. Having a cat.

But first, he said I had to check around. To see if
someone lost Mouse.

I got some cardboard and wrote

FounD
Gray kitten
555-3449

I put Mouse in a basket and we put up the sign.

Mr. Barker read it. He looked in the basket.

"Cute little thing."

He went back to pulling weeds.

"Did you lose him?" I asked.

"No," he said. "But I lost my weeder."

Mary Alice was his weeder. She helped him. And he paid her.

Mrs. O'Connor looked in the basket too.

"Is this that scruffy stray cat?" she asked.

I nodded and Mouse purred.

"It doesn't look scruffy now. With the right food, it won't be so scrawny either."

I looked at George. But not too much food, I thought.

Willie Martin pulled Mouse's tail.

Mouse scratched him.

He started to bawl and Mrs. Martin came running.

"Does that cat have its shots?" she asked.

I made a list of things we needed.

food
shots

Dad and I went to the store and got a box of
kitten food.

We found Mouse on Dad's desk when we got back.
There were papers scattered on the floor and a puddle
in the middle of them.

Dad groaned. "We forgot a litter box."

While Dad cleaned up the mess, I fixed lunch.
For Mouse and Dad and me.

CHAPTER EIGHT
. . . .

To the Vet

Mrs. O'Connor gave us the name of her vet and we took Mouse in.

The vet said Mouse was a he.

The vet gave him shots. And cleaned his ears. And told us how much food to give him.

Then the vet said, "Kittens like to play. They like to climb in paper bags. And chase balls of string.

"Kittens like lots of attention."

"I'm good at playing," I said.

We paid the bill, and Dad groaned again. "This is going to be expensive."

Mouse was sleeping when we got home, so I left him in his basket and went to see Mr. Barker.

"Mary Alice told me all about weeding," I said. "I can do her job while she's gone."

Mr. Barker put me right to work. When I finished, he paid me.

"Come over tomorrow morning and you can do the watering too," he said.

I went right home and showed Dad the money. "To pay for Mouse," I said.

Dad's whole face sparkled with a smile. "Mouse is lucky to have a girl like you," he said. "And so am I."

Mouse was sitting in the sun, licking his fur.
He purred when he saw me and came over and rubbed
against my leg. He felt warm and soft.

I got a paper bag.

Mouse crawled inside.

He poked his paw out and batted the air. Then he
pulled it in quick.

Dad heard me laughing and came to watch.

Then Dad poked his hand around the edge of the bag.

Mouse batted Dad's hand. Dad laughed too.

That night for dinner, Dad ordered Chinese take-out.
To celebrate, he said.

Mouse celebrated too. He licked the bottom of the carton.

Dad told Mom about Mouse when she called.

When he gave me the phone, Mom said, "I'll be able to see Mouse soon."

I didn't answer.

"Dad said you were worrying that I might stay in Colorado."

"I was," I said.

"I'm counting the days till I get home."

"I am too," I said.

"Tell me more about Mouse," Mom said.

"He purrs like a machine," I told her. "He's happy here."

"Sounds like you're taking good care of him."

I thought about making lunch for Dad and Mouse and getting a job to earn money. I thought about Dad cleaning up the mess and taking Mouse and me to the vet. I thought about us laughing and playing with Mouse.

"We're all taking good care of each other," I said.

CHAPTER NINE

Willie Learns About Cats

On Friday we took care of Willie Martin.

Mrs. Martin had to take Kyle to get his ears checked. Willie didn't want to go along.

"I brought my dump truck," Willie said.

We went to the back yard and loaded the truck with gravel.

I set some big rocks in a row. "These can be the houses," I said. "You can dump the gravel to make a street."

Mouse sat in the sun watching us.

After three loads of gravel, Willie said, "Let's give your kitty a ride."

He grabbed Mouse. Mouse hissed and kicked with his back legs, trying to get away.

Willie let go with a shriek and Mouse ran under the back porch.

Willie held out his hand to me. I saw the scratches.

"You can wash it off in the house," I said.

Willie stared at me. I guess he thought I would fuss like his mother does. He stopped crying and followed me to the bathroom.

"Mouse doesn't like me," he said as he dried his hands.

"Mouse might like you if you gave him a chance," I said. "I'll show you how to treat cats."

We went out and sat in the grass. "Cats are curious," I said. "And they like to chase things."

I trailed my finger through the grass. I saw Mouse watching. I made the grass wiggle. Mouse crouched down and wiggled his back end. Willie laughed.

Then Mouse pounced. He caught my hand and tumbled on his back.

"Can I try?" Willie asked.

I nodded.

Mouse caught Willie's hand too.

When Mrs. Martin came to get Willie, Mouse was purring in his lap.

"Come and play with Mouse another day," I told Willie as he left.

Both Dad and Mrs. Martin looked surprised. I just smiled.

CHAPTER TEN
• • • • • • • • • • •
Summer Fun

The last week went by fast.

Willie came over one afternoon to play with Mouse. I couldn't find the string, so we took a newspaper outside and spread it out for Mouse to crawl under.

Mouse made tunnels under the pages. Then he peeked out and watched us.

I tore off a corner of one page and crumpled it into a ball. When I rolled it across the grass Mouse chased it.

"Can we teach him to fetch?" Willie asked.

"Let's try," I said.

Willie started crumpling paper too. Mouse chased balls everywhere.

Then Mouse dropped one of the balls in front of Willie.

"He did it," Willie said. "Mouse is the smartest cat in the whole world.

Mouse just ran off to pounce on another ball.

"Here, Mouse," Willie called. "Bring it here."

"I think he'll only bring it when he wants to," I said. "Smart cats are like that."

Afterward we went over to Willie's. We played on the swings and set up a camp under the willow tree.

Mrs. Martin brought us a snack in our camp.

Friday when I got home from Mr. Barker's, Dad was typing with one hand and petting Mouse with the other.

"C'mon, Mouse," I said. And we went into the kitchen to make peanut butter sandwiches. I peeled some carrots too.

"I'm not mad at Mom anymore," I told Dad when I gave him his lunch.

"Were you mad?" he asked.

I nodded. "I didn't want her to leave. I didn't want it to be summer. I wasn't having any fun."

"Are you having fun now?" Dad asked.

"Yes," I said, "because I have Mouse."

"I'm glad you found each other," Dad said.

That afternoon Dad and I cleaned house. Mom would be home tomorrow.

We twisted crepe paper around the doorways. Mouse helped with that job. Crepe paper got twisted around him too.

I made a big sign.

WeLcome Home!

Dad and I wrote our names with the paintbrush. I stuck Mouse's front foot in the paint and he made a pawprint on the sign.

"We can save this for Justin," Dad said, "since he'll be back next week."

Justin didn't know about Mouse yet. "I can't wait for him to meet Mouse," I said.

When we finished doing all our chores, Dad asked, "Shall we eat out? To celebrate our last night?"

I shook my head. "Let's cook dinner together."

Dad found a recipe for spaghetti.

I washed the lettuce and tore it into little chunks.

We used the good dishes. Dad said it was okay for Mouse to use one of the good dishes too.

We raised our glasses. "To summer fun," Dad said.

"To Mouse," I said.

"To Mom coming home," Dad said.

"To Mom coming home," I repeated.

After dinner we washed the dishes and put everything away.

Then we sat on the back porch and watched the twilight gather.

Mouse chased fireflies. He disappeared into the shadows and we crept after him.

We found him under the currant bush, licking his fur. He looked up at me and yawned. I yawned too.

"Time for bed," Dad said.

We went inside.

"Thanks for taking such good care of me," Dad said.
He tucked the covers under my chin.
"Thanks for taking such good care of *me*," I said back.
Mouse just wiggled against my feet and purred.